This book
belongs to:

Barbie™

Sweet Treats

Barbie and her sisters are going to have a party. First of all they must go shopping to buy provisions.

"Gosh, these bags are so heavy!" says Barbie.

"Yes, but we've got all the things we need to bake some delicious cakes," says Stacie with excitement.

When the girls arrive home, they lay out all the ingredients they will need for baking.

"You must show us what to do, Barbie," says Skipper. "I don't know where to begin!"

Barbie fetches some aprons for them to wear to protect their clothes.

"Right," she says. "Let's get organised. We'll be the greatest baking team ever!"

"What shall we make first?" asks Barbie.

"Let's do the fudge cakes," says Skipper. "They sound so delicious."

The girls check the recipe to see what they need.

"Stacie, please could you pass me the electric whisk? Then I will show you how to whisk the egg whites," says Barbie.

Skipper passes the eggs to Barbie very carefully.

"It would be awful if they broke all over the floor!" she says.

When all the ingredients are ready, Barbie and Skipper start to mix them all together in a bowl, while Stacie whisks the eggs.

"Now we need to put the cakes in the oven for half an hour," says Barbie.

Later, the girls take the cakes out of the oven.

"Wow! They look fantastic!" says Skipper.

"Please can I be the first to have a taste?" cries Stacie. "I will be the official taster!"

"We'll allow you one cake as a special treat," laughs Barbie. "But first we must let them cool and then the paper cases can be peeled off."

Stacie thinks that baking is great fun.

"Let's make the next cake!" she says.

Barbie smiles. "I'm glad you are enjoying it so much. This time we need to put the cake in the fridge to set."

After lots of mixing and whisking, Stacie proudly puts the cake into the fridge.

"Let's leave it in there for an hour," says Barbie.

A little while later, Ken arrives with baby Tommy to help the girls get ready for the party.

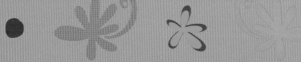

"Goodness, you've been busy!" says Ken. "It looks like a cake shop in here."

It is time for Stacie to take the cake out of the fridge.

"Ooh, can I have a taste?" says Ken.

"Only if you blow up some party balloons for us," laughs Barbie.

So Ken helps the girls to get everything ready for the party.

"Perhaps you and Tommy could lay everything out on the table for us," suggests Skipper.

"But where *is* Tommy?" asks Stacie.

"Oh no! He's found the icing for our cake!" says Barbie.

"Hey, Tommy!" says Ken. "You'll get a tummy ache if you eat all of that! Come and help me lay the table for the party."

So Ken lifts Tommy onto his shoulder, while Barbie and Skipper finish icing the cakes.

At last, everything is ready. The cakes are spread out on the table and the guests arrive for the party.

"Wow! These cakes are amazing!"

Nobody can resist having a taste of every cake.

"Well, I wouldn't have been able to do it without all my helpers," says Barbie, smiling.

"We're the best baking team ever, thanks to you, Barbie!" laughs Skipper.

"Who knows? Perhaps we'll open our very own cake shop one day!"